Hooray! Hooray!
I sit! I stay!

ALADDIN
An imprint of Simon & Schuster Children's Publishing Division
1230 Avenue of the Americas, New York, New York 10020
This Aladdin hardcover edition December 2019
Text copyright © 2016 by Mick Inkpen
Illustrations copyright © 2016 by Chloë Inkpen
Published by arrangement with Hodder and Stoughton
Originally published as *Fred* in Great Britain in 2016 by Hodder Children's Books, a division of Hachette Children's Group
All rights reserved, including the right of reproduction in whole or in part in any form.
ALADDIN and related logo are registered trademarks of Simon & Schuster, Inc.
For information about special discounts for bulk purchases, please contact Simon & Schuster Special Sales at
1-866-506-1949 or business@simonandschuster.com.
The Simon & Schuster Speakers Bureau can bring authors to your live event. For more information or to book an event contact
the Simon & Schuster Speakers Bureau at 1-866-248-3049 or visit our website at www.simonspeakers.com.
The text of this book was set in 1533 GLC Augereau Pro.
Manufactured in China 0919 HUI
2 4 6 8 10 9 7 5 3 1
Library of Congress Control Number 2019931779
ISBN 978-1-5344-1475-4 (hc)
ISBN 978-1-5344-1476-1 (eBook)

I love you, Fred

by Mick Inkpen
illustrated by Chloë Inkpen

ALADDIN
New York   London   Toronto   Sydney   New Delhi

I am not the best in class.
But I'm not last!
I passed my test
along with all the rest.
When called to come,
I do not run away!

(Not often, anyway.)

And I can fetch a stick
or ball.
I come when called.
And that's not all. . . .

I sit! I stay!

I do not
run away.

Hooray!

"Fetch!"
     and "Sit!"
and "Stay!"
     I understand them all.
Those are the words I know.

And "Ball!"
     and "Walk!"
and "Park!"
     and "Bed!"
I know those, too.

But what is . . .

. . . "Fred"?

"Fred! Fred! Fred!" they say.
They say it all the time.
  "Fred! Fred! Fred!" all day.
(You whisper it sometimes.)

If only I could Fred.

If I can Fetch and Sit and Stay,
I'll Fred. I know I will.
  And they will clap and say,
"Good Boy!"

I know they will.

There is another dog upstairs
where I am not allowed to go.
  I saw him once.
I wonder if he knows
what Fred is all about
and why they shout it
  all the time.

He looks like me!
He has my ball.
  He has no smell at all.

I'm chasing pigeons in the park,
which I am not allowed to do.
I like the way they flap about.
I think they like it too.

And if there are

no pigeons, a duck will have to do!

There is that other
dog again!
The dog I saw
the other day!
And look!
He has my ball again!
I wonder if he wants to . . .

play!

Paddle!

Struggle!

Bubble!

Trouble!

Kick!

And splutter!

Choke!

And sink . . .

"Fred!"

I hear.
But cannot think.

A scream!

A dash!

A jump!

A splash!

A foot!

A face . . .

It's you!
I'm safe!

"Oh, Fred," you whisper.
"Fred. Fred. Fred."

A light goes on
inside my head!

Fred is a **name**!

Fred
is my
name!

And suddenly I see
that I am Fred!
That Fred . . .

. . . is **me!**

I have been Fredding
all the time!
Fred is a name.

And it is **mine!**

I whiz around. . . .

. . . I lift my paw.

Then jump into
your arms once more.

There's nothing left
for me to do,
except to run
back home
with you.

I drag my blanket
from my bed
and snuggle up
with you instead.

I think
the thought
inside my head
that **knows**
that I am . . .

. . . Fred.